FOR
SEBASTIAN WALKER
WHO STIRRED IT all up
FOR The Best.

Copyright © 1993 by John Burningham

All rights reserved.

First U.S. edition 1993

Published in Great Britain in 1993 by Walker Books Ltd., London.

Library of Congress Cataloging-in-Publication Data

Burningham, John.

Harvey Slumfenburger's Christmas present / John Burningham.—
1st U.S. ed.

Summary: On discovering late Christmas Eve that he has forgotten
to deliver one present, Santa Claus wearily makes his way in a variety of conveyances
to the top of the Roly Poly Mountains to deliver it.

ISBN 1-56402-246-3

1. Santa Claus—Juvenile fiction.   [1. Santa Claus—Fiction.
2. Christmas—Fiction.   3. Vehicles—Fiction.]   I. Title.

PZ7.B936Har   1993   92–54957

[E]—dc20

10 9 8 7 6 5 4 3 2 1

Printed in Italy

The pictures in this book were done in pen and watercolor.

Candlewick Press
2067 Massachusetts Avenue
Cambridge, Massachusetts 02140

Harvey Slumfenburger's
Christmas
Present

John Burningham

CANDLEWICK PRESS

CAMBRIDGE, MASSACHUSETTS

It was Christmas Eve.
Santa Claus and the
reindeer were home at last.
They were very tired because
they had been delivering presents
to all the children everywhere.

They had something to eat,
and then Santa put the reindeer
to bed. One of the reindeer said
it did not feel very well—maybe
it had nibbled something on the
way that it should not have.

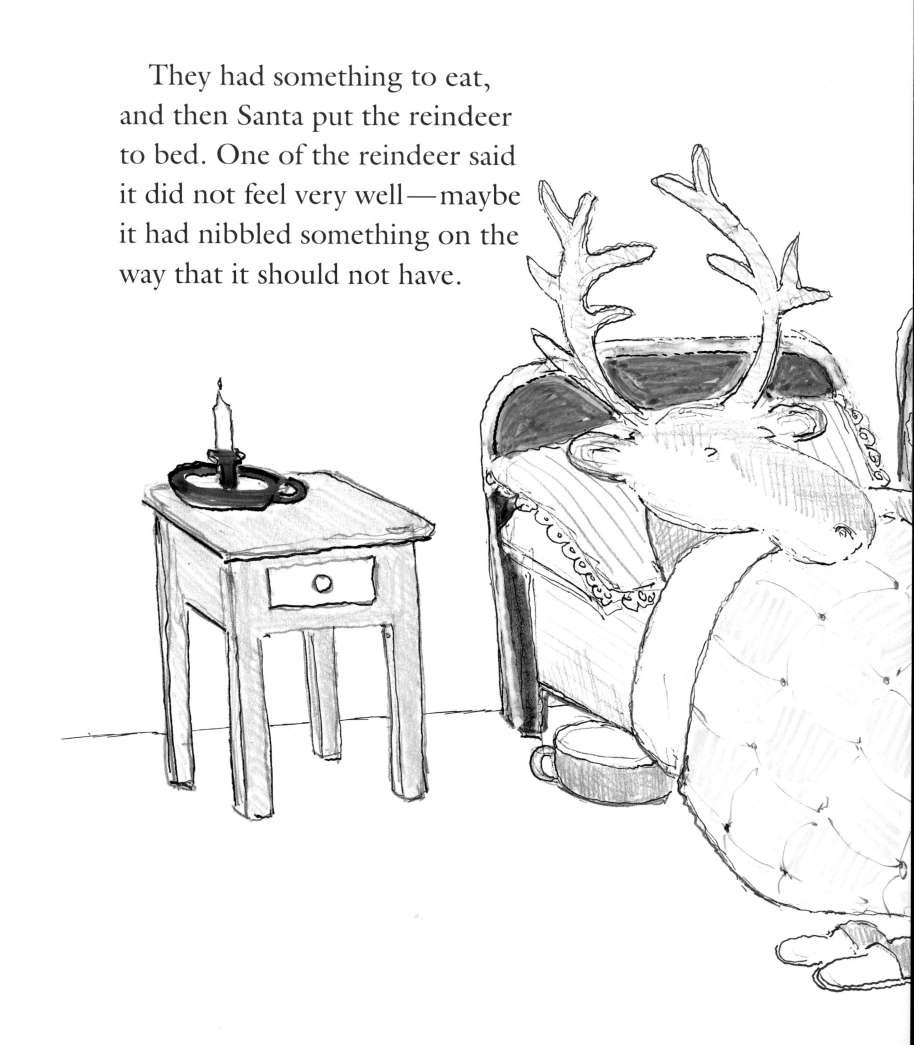

Santa thought that all
it needed was a good
night's sleep.

Finally Santa was able to go to bed. He put on his pajamas and was just climbing into bed when he saw something that made him gasp. At the end of his bed lay his sack. Santa could see the shape of one present still inside it.

Santa pulled the present out of the sack. The present was Harvey Slumfenburger's.

Santa knew all about Harvey Slumfenburger. He knew that Harvey Slumfenburger's parents were too poor to buy him presents. He knew that Harvey Slumfenburger only ever got one present, and that was the present that Santa brought him. He knew that Harvey Slumfenburger lived in a hut at the top of the Roly Poly Mountain, which was far, far away.

Santa was very tired.
The reindeer were asleep, and one of
them was not very well. But Santa knew he
had to get the present to Harvey Slumfenburger.

Santa put on his coat over his pajamas. He put
on his boots and hat, picked up the sack with Harvey
Slumfenburger's present in it, and started to walk

through the cold winter night to the hut where
Harvey Slumfenburger lived at the top of the
Roly Poly Mountain, which was far, far away.

Santa had not gone very far when he met a man with an airplane. "Excuse me," he said, "my name is Santa Claus. I still have one present left in my sack, which is for Harvey Slumfenburger, the little boy who lives in a hut at the top of the Roly Poly Mountain, which is far, far away. And it will soon be Christmas Day."

"Get in my plane," said the man, "and I will take you as far as I can." The airplane took off and flew through the night sky toward the Roly Poly Mountain.

Heavy snow began to fall.

"I am so sorry, Santa," said the man. "I cannot fly my airplane any farther in this snow." The plane bumped and skidded across the ground and finally came to a halt. "But if you go to the garage that lies over the hill, there is a man with a jeep. Maybe he can help you."

Santa set off through the snow. He went over the hill to the garage where there was the man with the jeep. "Excuse me," he said, "my name is Santa Claus. I still have one present left in my sack, which is for Harvey Slumfenburger, the little boy who lives in a hut at the top of the Roly Poly Mountain, which is far, far away. And it will soon be Christmas Day."

"Climb in my jeep," said the man, "and I will take you as far as I can."

The jeep bounced and spun across the fields and down the road toward the Roly Poly Mountain.

But then the jeep skidded and crashed through the fence and into a tree. Santa was sent tumbling into the snow.

"I am so sorry, Santa," said the man. "I can take you no farther. But if you go down the hill and across the river, there is a boy with a motorbike. Maybe he can help you."

Santa went down the hill and across the river and met the boy with the motorbike. "Excuse me," he said, "my name is Santa Claus. I still have one present left in my sack, which is for Harvey Slumfenburger, the little boy who lives in a hut at the top of the Roly Poly Mountain, which is far, far away. And it will soon be Christmas Day."

"We'll go on my motorbike," said the boy. "I will take you as far as I can."

The motorbike roared off along the road toward the Roly Poly Mountain.

But they had not gone very far before the
motorbike slid on some ice and they both fell off.
"I am so sorry, Santa," said the boy. "The front
of my bike is all twisted, and I can take you no
farther. But if you go across the valley and
into the woods, there is a girl who has skis.
Maybe she can help you."

Santa went across the valley and into the woods, where he found the girl with skis. "Excuse me," he said, "my name is Santa Claus. I still have one present left in my sack, which is for Harvey Slumfenburger, the little boy who lives in a hut at the top of the Roly Poly Mountain, which is far, far away. And it will soon be Christmas Day."

"Stand on the back of my skis," said the girl, "and I will take you as far as I can toward the Roly Poly Mountain."

They had not gone very far when the skis broke
with a crack and they both tumbled into the snow.

"I am so sorry, Santa," said the girl. "My skis are broken and I can take you no farther. But if you go up the slope and down onto the plain, you will be near the bottom of the Roly Poly Mountain, where there is a climber with a rope. Maybe he can help you."

Santa went up the slope and down onto the plain, where he found the climber with the rope. "Excuse me," he said, "my name is Santa Claus. I still have one present left in my sack, which is for Harvey Slumfenburger, the little boy who lives in a hut at the top of the Roly Poly Mountain, which is far, far away. And it will soon be Christmas Day."

"Hold on to my rope," said the climber, "and I will take you as far as I can up the Roly Poly Mountain."

They had not climbed very far when the rope broke, and Santa nearly fell off the Roly Poly Mountain. "I am so sorry, Santa," said the climber. "My rope is broken and I cannot climb any higher. But if you keep going up that cliff and over those boulders, you will see a little hut at the top, and that is the hut where Harvey Slumfenburger lives."

Santa kept going up the cliff and over the
boulders and finally arrived at the hut where
Harvey Slumfenburger lived.

Santa climbed
onto the roof
and down
the chimney…

and put the present in Harvey Slumfenburger's stocking.

Then Santa set
off on the long
journey home.

Santa checked
that the reindeer
were all right and
tucked in bed.

And as the sun began to rise on Christmas morning, Santa climbed into bed and was soon fast asleep.

In the hut at the top of the Roly Poly Mountain, which is far, far away, a little boy, whose name was Harvey Slumfenburger, reached for the stocking on the end of his bed and took out his present.

I wonder what it was.